In
1935 if you wanted to
read a good book, you needed
either a lot of money or a library card.
Cheap paperbacks were available, but their
poor production generally mirrored the quality
between the covers. One weekend that year,
Allen Lane, Managing Director of The Bodley Head,
having spent the weekend visiting Agatha Christie,
found himself on a platform at Exeter station trying to
find something to read for his journey back to London.
He was appalled by the quality of the material he had to
choose from. Everything that Allen Lane achieved from that
day until his death in 1970 was based on a passionate belief
in the existence of 'a vast reading public for *intelligent*
books at a low price'. The result of his momentous vision
was the birth not only of Penguin, but of the 'paperback
revolution'. Quality writing became available for the price of
a packet of cigarettes, literature became a mass medium
for the first time, a nation of book-borrowers became a
nation of book-buyers – and the very concept of book
publishing was changed for ever. Those founding
principles – of quality and value, with an overarching
belief in the fundamental importance of reading –
have guided everything the company has
done since 1935. Sir Allen Lane's
pioneering spirit is still very much alive
at Penguin in 2005. Here's to
the next 70 years!

MORE THAN A BUSINESS

'We decided it was time to end the almost customary half-hearted manner in which cheap editions were produced – as though the only people who could possibly want cheap editions must belong to a lower order of intelligence. We, however, believed in the existence in this country of a vast reading public for intelligent books at a low price, and staked everything on it'
Sir Allen Lane, 1902–1970

'The Penguin Books are splendid value for sixpence, so splendid that if other publishers had any sense they would combine against them and suppress them'
George Orwell

'More than a business ... a national cultural asset'
Guardian

'When you look at the whole Penguin achievement you know that it constitutes, in action, one of the more democratic successes of our recent social history'
Richard Hoggart

On Shopping

INDIA KNIGHT

PENGUIN BOOKS

PENGUIN BOOKS

Published by the Penguin Group
Penguin Books Ltd, 80 Strand, London WC2R ORL, England
Penguin Group (USA) Inc., 375 Hudson Street, New York, New York 10014, USA
Penguin Group (Canada), 10 Alcorn Avenue, Toronto, Ontario, Canada M4V 3B2
(a division of Pearson Penguin Canada Inc.)
Penguin Ireland, 25 St Stephen's Green, Dublin 2, Ireland
(a division of Penguin Books Ltd)
Penguin Group (Australia), 250 Camberwell Road, Camberwell, Victoria 3124,
Australia (a division of Pearson Australia Group Pty Ltd)
Penguin Books India Pvt Ltd, 11 Community Centre,
Panchsheel Park, New Delhi – 110 017, India
Penguin Group (NZ), cnr Airborne and Rosedale Roads, Albany,
Auckland 1310, New Zealand (a division of Pearson New Zealand Ltd)
Penguin Books (South Africa) (Pty) Ltd, 24 Sturdee Avenue,
Rosebank 2196, South Africa

Penguin Books Ltd, Registered Offices: 80 Strand, London WC2R ORL, England

www.penguin.com

'Beginning', 'Looking Better' and 'Mothers and Children'
first published in *The Shops*, Viking 2003
Published in Penguin Books 2004
'New in Store' first published 2005
This selection published as a Pocket Penguin 2005

1

Copyright © India Knight, 2003, 2004, 2005
All rights reserved

The moral right of the author has been asserted

Set in 11/13pt Monotype Dante
Typeset by Palimpsest Book Production Limited
Polmont, Stirlingshire
Printed in England by Clays Ltd, St Ives plc

Contents

Beginning

It saddens and amazes me that there are people out there who actually hate shopping. Men, for instance, are traditionally supposed to be hopeless at it: grumpy and monosyllabic when lured down the high street, wishing they were at home browsing the web for gadgets instead. Now, I don't want to come over all American self-help manual here (pity – I'd probably have a best-seller on my hands if I did: *Because You're Worth It – How to Shop for the Self within You*), but hating shopping is a terrible accident. It happens to people who've never shopped properly, and allow one bad experience to contaminate and sully the rest of their shopping life. It is extremely sad, a) because it just is and b) because we all *have* to shop, whether we like it or not. So we may as well like it. Even heterosexual blokes.

I can see how it happens, though, shop-hatred. Devoted as I am to my number one hobby, it would be plain foolish not to admit that some shopping experiences are absolutely hellish. I am thinking of Oxford Street on a Saturday afternoon: swarms of people not knowing what they want but knowing they want it badly, milling around like grubs (I'm mixing my metaphors, but they're all to do with insects, you'll notice); the smell of cheap burgers; the rustle of nyloned thigh meeting nyloned thigh; the sense of despair; the grotesque, palpable greed . . . Yes, it's hell. But this scenario has as little to do with true shopping as a drunken fumble in an alleyway with a man who looks like a pig has to do with a weekend at the Ritz with the one you love. We'll get to that later. We'll make every shopping experience as far removed from the icky fumble as is humanly possible. It's not difficult when you know how – but it's not necessarily easy to know how, either. For many of us – well, many of *you* – shopping is simply bewildering. It promises, but it doesn't deliver. There is a literal embarrassment of choice. And so shopping becomes joyless.

But first we need to go back to the beginning. Where does it come from, this delight in The Shops? Is it inherited? Is there a shopping gene? Certainly, my mother was – and remains – a champion shopper. But, possibly because of her ultra-luxe tastes, when I was a child she shopped in a very different way from me. Put simply, I like tat and the romance of tat – of stupid, pointless, lovely, glittery cheap things – and she doesn't. She didn't shop very frequently, but when she did, you knew about it. I shop little and often, a method I strongly recommend.

Beginning

When I was a small girl, growing up in Brussels
with frequent exeats to Paris, we seemed to be
either improbably rich or improbably hard up, with
no in-betweens. My parents separated when I was
two, and my mother and I lived by ourselves in a
(for the time) freakily minimalist apartment on the
Avenue de Tervuren. My mother, a designer who
is blessed with a most extraordinary 'eye', has
always had minimal tastes, and so there we were,
with acres of bareness (lack of funds may have
contributed to the overall look), the odd exquisite
objet and a fascinating textured blue rubber floor
that looked like giant bubble wrap in our kitchen.
We ate porridge when we were broke, which was
about half the time, and tins and tins of sardines
('full of protein', though I think the aesthetic aspect
– the beautiful retro Spanish and Portuguese labels
on the tins – had as much to do with it as the nutri-
tional one). When we weren't broke . . . well, my
mother tells a story which I think I am supposed
to be obscurely flattered by, which in reality I find
crippling, but which I pass on anyway in the spirit
of explanation. I was aged about five, and she about
twenty-three, and we were in an upmarket Brussels
supermarket called Rob – a kind of Belgian
Fortnum's, now defunct – and as we were queu-
ing up to pay, she remembers me panickedly telling
her, at the top of my voice, that we'd forgotten
the caviare: *Maman, maman, on a oublié le caviare.*

3

One can only imagine the delight of the other shoppers.

So that was my mother: feast or famine. Sardines with crunchy, spindly bones or Beluga for two. I have no recollection whatsoever of buying Jif or loo paper or potatoes with her, though surely we must have done. All my shopping memories of my mother involve things like haring around looking for Alfonso mangoes (they're only in season for one month); buying hundreds of postcards of the head of Nefertiti when the Tutankhamun exhibition hit Brussels in the 1970s; and buying clothes.

Ah, the clothes. We were very well dressed, my mother and I (she still is. I am writing this in fleecy pyjama bottoms and an ancient, dog-smelling jumper). When she married my stepfather and we came to live in England, in crazy, beyond-parody 1970s Islington (in Sisterwrite, the local bookshop, an alarm bell sounded if a man walked in), I remember one of the mothers of the children on the square talking disapprovingly about my 'funny French clothes'. Even then, aged ten, I felt some pity for the woman in question, rather than any deep sense of hurt for myself: dungareed, braless and make-upless, with hair like rats' tails – to say nothing of a crashing lack of manners – I knew she could really have benefited from my clothes-related (and, by this time, cosmetic) knowledge. God, those middle-class women. As though looking ugly made you Of The People. Anyway – I was shy and only just learning English, and so I didn't say anything, but it didn't stop me from thinking to myself that she had hands like raw hams and that a good blow-dry wouldn't have gone amiss, to say nothing of a slick of mascara and some decent lingerie. She needed The Shops, poor her, and she didn't know how. (At the time, the idea of anyone ingeniously making a political statement against patriarchy – we are wimmin and so on – simply by looking hideous didn't occur to me. I just felt sorry.)

There was a shop in Brussels called Dujardin, where all my *bon-chic-bon-genre* clothes came from: grey flannel pinafore dresses, pleated navy-blue woollen skirts, pastelly jerseys and heaps of that faux-Brit kit – duffle coats, kilts, tweedy things – that sends well-off Europeans into ecstasies (it still makes me smile – or wince in recognition – to see young French men of a certain kind wearing very neat jeans, brogues, a stripy shirt and a pale yellow cashmere jumper tied nonchalantly around their shoulders: *le style Anglais*, never seen *en Angleterre* ever. It's like upper-middle-class French children being called Kevin or Bryan: sweet, and not entirely uncomical).

Anyway, so there I was, in my clothes. For a while, in Brussels, I went to the local primary school, where I had a lovely time but was fairly acutely aware of my outfits, which were not like the clothes of other children. My best friend,

Cécile, wore platform shoes, tiny broderie-anglaise tops with puffed sleeves, and miniskirts. She had long, wild-looking sort of hair; I had a chic crop (which would have been more chic had my ears not stuck out bonkersly and had I not looked like a boy – a young, curly-locked Greek shepherd boy, to be precise) and *the* most conservative, ankle-skimming, top-button-done-up wardrobe imaginable. But I was happy in my navy-blue cardigans and casual weekend corduroys, even though, thirty years later, I am sniggering to think of myself then.

Thrown into the mix was the fact that my mother kept running away to India and to Pakistan with me in tow. So in April there I'd be, Little Miss Square, and in May I'd be running around barefoot in a shalwaar kameez, bugging my grandmother to pierce my nose (which she eventually did, in the garden, with a red-hot sewing needle). And then we'd go back to Brussels – except once, when war broke out and we were stuck for several months; my grandmother showed me how to tie a sari and cook parathas as the bombs fell nearby, leaving huge craters (melodramatic, but true). Usually, though, it'd be a see-saw between the bliss of being hot in the sunshine in thin cotton clothing and the equal bliss (hmmm, kind of) of being cold in Belgium, swathed in itchy wool.

Having got my nose pierced by one grandmother – I snorted the earring-back by mistake and had to be held upside down, choking, until I coughed it up again, after which we let the hole close up – I thought I'd try my other granny for a few shopping expeditions. What I really wanted was a top with little puff sleeves like my friend Cécile. My mother, alas, had decided that such tops were tarty – and, looking back, Cécile didn't exactly exude wholesomeness, possibly because she had mini-bosoms. Of course, unwholesomeness is what you absolutely die for if you're a precocious child aware of her own squareness – and mini-bosoms too, ideally. So I set about persuading my grandmother. She had a house at the Belgian seaside, in a place called Le Zoute, and there, across from the promenade by the beach, was a shop called Princess, and in its window was a pale pink puff-sleeved top in fluffy angora. The shop itself was shockingly expensive, and patronized solely by small blonde girls who wore those coats with velvet collars in the winter. In the summers, at the beach, they wore designer bikinis and had lithe, elongated tennis-club limbs. There was something terrifying about those little girls – something arctic and Grace Kelly-like that was totally intimidating and used to make me feel as though I was a tinker just off the encampment. They weren't mean or anything – one, Jessica, became my closest summer-holidays friend for about ten years: we used to walk to Holland together, along the beach, eat waffles at the café as soon as we got there and race back, stuffed, to beat the tide. But the way those girls looked – glacial and hot at the same time, like sexy Nazis – really gave me the willies on the one hand, and made me sick with jealousy on the other. Princess was where they all shopped.

The shop was daunting. It had enormous windows, with very few clothes on display: each 'piece' was shown as though it were a priceless jewel. My grandmother balked at the price of the angora jumper with puffy sleeves in the window, but I dragged her back again and again to stare at it, until, eventually, we went in. I can't remember if this was before or after the family firm, which made wallpaper (and had once employed Magritte as a designer, oddly), had gone bankrupt through the financial naiveté of my great-grandfather's six daughters, but I think it must have been afterwards, because my grandmother, her income suddenly slashed and replaced by a certain temporary chippiness, didn't like being there at all. This sort of shop had been her natural habitat, but she couldn't really afford it any more. I was certainly aware of this, but I really wanted the top with the puffy sleeves and so, manipulative minx that I was, I pretended not to notice. The shop assistants were snooty: my granny's fur coat had seen better days and I looked like a brown boy with sticky-out ears and Greek hair. Buying the top was not a comfortable experience – it made me want to pee with anxiety – but I remember swanning out of the shop with my navy-and-white Princess carrier bag (little crown above the 'i') feeling nothing short of ecstatic. I wore that top until it quite literally fell apart. And so I learned my first lesson about boutique shopping: it's scary, but only the first time. And, observing my poor meek, smiling grandmother, I decided that if shop assistants are going to be rude to you, and you're not grand enough not to mind, the only course of action that's going to make you feel better is to be rude back.

So there you go. Not a particularly edifying story, but then one's behaviour tends not to be particularly edifying in moments of extreme Shops anguish. A good shop assistant would have made my grandmother feel pleased to be in such an elegant shop, pleased to be parting with money she didn't have, pleased all round, really. (Obviously, a good child wouldn't have dragged her impecunious grandmother into such a shop in the first place. I *know*.) A really good shop assistant is like a soft mugger: he takes all your stuff, but very gently, cooing at you that your bag is divine, and then he gives you a quick metaphorical shoulder massage afterwards, so that you leave feeling displeased (no wallet left to speak of) but also strangely relaxed, strangely woozy and almost post-coital.

My mother is the rudest woman I know if shop assistants fail to please. Normally, of course, she is perfectly charming, and makes a point of being nice to them, especially if they are beautiful, or seem unhappy/poor, or are brunettes (we all have our prejudices). And she's been friends with the cashiers at her local branch of Sainsbury's for pretty much thirty years, greeting them all by name and having huge long chats. But if sales assistants are crap at their job and uninterested, or – God forbid – crap at their job, uninterested and *very glossy* (certain shops specialize in producing these, which I think is a mistake: you don't want your sales girl yawning and showing her expensive veneers while swathed in clouds of cashmere) . . . well, we're talking nuclear.

First, my mother raises an eyebrow – a particularly glacial eyebrow: its arc says, with stunning eloquence, 'You are just so unbelievably ghastly.' (I long to be able to do this with my eyebrow, but I just end up looking like I'm doing Roger Moore. Eyebrows matter almost more than anything else in your face, by the way.)

Being on the receiving end of the eyebrow is startling enough. Hitherto bored, manicure-examining sales girls who have been busy sneering at your shoes and thinking your bag is very last season suddenly stand up straight, stare around them nervously and get that look animals do when they know for a fact that a bigger animal is going to eat them – the vole meets stoat look, if you will. But it's too late! They should have paid attention earlier! The stoat is heading in for the kill, and the vole, in one horrible blinding moment of realization, knows it's her little bones that are about to be snapped.

Post-eyebrow, we get an 'Excuse me?' so filled with disbelief and contempt that, really, it sends shivers down the sturdiest spines. When I was a teenager, out shopping with my mother, this was the point at which I would endeavour to disappear. The Excuse Me inevitably provokes stammering in the person to whom it is addressed, and it is not comfortable to watch – nature red in tooth and claw, and so on.

After the Excuse Me, and the gibbering, wet-palmed responses it provokes, we get the attack proper, the vocabulary of which is innocuous enough: 'Could you please explain to me why I have been waiting for twenty minutes to find out if you have these in a Medium / waiting for you to stop chatting to your friend / waiting for service', etc. etc. The attack is delivered smoothly and softly – the stoat, after all, dispatches its vole victim swiftly and does not toy with it. The sales assistant is nearly in tears. My mother then asks to speak to the manager.

My mother's intolerance in the face of bad service is founded on two basic principles: a) that there is nothing wrong in working in the service industry and b) that if a job's worth doing, it's worth doing well. Having had a series of rubbish jobs for which I was paid grotesquely small amounts of money, I can't entirely concur, and so I can't do Vole–Stoat very well (there have been exceptions). But a friend and I, having been treated like we were two poos in frocks by an especially unlovely sales assistant in Brompton Cross, once came up with an excellent, idiot-proof alternative. It's not Vole–Stoat, but it *is* pretty good. You stand there, feeling small and shabby and dissed, and then, as you're about to leave, you say to the (female) shop assistant, quite loudly,

YOU HAVE A MOUSTACHE.

You don't laugh: you are a compassionate fellow woman, offering advice. If you think you can manage it, you can wave your index finger around your upper lip a little, to illustrate, and make a little sad moue of sympathy. And then you leave.

I've completely digressed, though you'll thank me one day for the moustache tip. I was trying to ascertain whether there was such a thing as a shopping gene. This is kind of unlikely, I'll grant you – but I do believe that a love of shops is, as with so many other things, bred in the bone. If you think it's normal to go into ecstasies over sugar tongs, tennis shoes, crayons, book bindings, chess pieces and Bic cigarette lighters, and if all of your nearest and dearest agree, then those ecstasies become part of you, and part of your response to the world.

My father loved the shops too; mostly he loved buying motorbikes. I have a marvellous photograph of him taken in the South of France, under an avenue of lime trees, leggily straddling his giant bike, his black leathers matching his black hair. He must have been in his mid-forties. He is smiling up at the sky, as though to thank Our Lord for Kawasakis. In fact, he loved buying motorbikes so much that he packed in his job one day and opened a bike shop. I used to spend half of the school holidays with him in Brussels, and he'd have me model all the bike jackets – I especially remember a make called Furygan which had a snarling black panther on the back. He'd tell me all about the leather, the stitching, what kind of impact the leathers could withstand. (He was interested in this, having nearly lost a leg after a particularly nasty crash – two years in hospital and amputation only just averted by my twenty-something mother giving the doctors a daily dose of Vole–Stoat Ultra.) He loved his bike shop, he was truly happy; but having no experience of trade whatsoever, he died a double bankrupt, his prized Bennelli long gone to pay off creditors. His biker buddies, now old and bikeless, sent a wreath to his funeral.

So I know my bikes quite well. I also know my shirts. My father had dozens in pink, yellow and lavender; most of them came from England. They used to hang in his closet in blocks of colour, crisp and starched and immaculate, and sometimes I used to stare at them for ages, feeling utterly contented, feeling that order was a very good thing, and represented by these shirts.

He loved clothes, my dad, nearly as much as bikes, and he used to take me shopping in the holidays (pre-bankruptcy). He was one of those men who used to love, and appreciate, all the women around him – his wives, of whom there were many over the years, his daughter, his mother – to be well dressed. He was the opposite of mean: if you liked the Benetton skirt in pink, he'd buy it in red and in orange for you too. Being the kind of man he was, he had a horror of unfemininity, which, in my case, translated itself into the purchasing of clothes – at my urging – that my mother wouldn't necessarily have approved of: short clothes, or clothes with *décolletages*, or clothes that somehow felt racy (though perhaps only to me, since one of these was, bewilderingly in retrospect, an apple-green velour top with a giant collar and even more giant zip). I was, naturally, in heaven. The only thing wrong with his shopping skills was that he was unnaturally keen on yellow, my least favourite colour. There is a slew of photographs of me as a child looking jaundiced in yellow coats and yellow hats and yellow boots.

When I last saw my father, in an old people's home in the Ardennes, he was dying of cancer and Alzheimer's. He was extremely badly dressed, in a horrible sweatshirt and floppy trousers – and the adult nappy had never been part of his repertoire before. He was completely gaga. I went outside and smoked twenty cigarettes and sobbed away to myself, and then I gave the nurse money to buy him decent clothes that fitted him. She said that his clothes were freshly laundered every day and that he didn't mind what he wore. I did Vole–Stoat: my mother's daughter, as well as my pink-and-lavender-shirted father's. When he died and I collected his things, there were two crisp new shirts, a new navy cardigan and two new pairs of brown cords in his wardrobe. And on his dressing table, there was a picture of me peering out grumpily in a canary-yellow anorak.

Looking Better

First off, I am not a beauty expert, though I am a beauty junkie. I did have a brief stint writing about beauty products, which I enjoyed tremendously, but I want to make it clear that I am not a beauty editor, have never worked in the beauty industry, don't specialize in writing about lip gloss – you get the picture. If you're after a genuine beauty bible, compiled and written by people who really know their stuff, get the accurately named *21st Century Beauty Bible*, by Sarah Stacey and Josephine Fairley. It is *bliss*, very useful, heaven to read in the bath, and packed to the gills with information. Their website is good too: www.thebeautybible.com.

Elsewhere, do please bear in mind that editorial coverage of beauty products in your favourite glossy magazine is inextricably and fundamentally linked to advertising, that no glossies can survive without advertising, *ergo* that if X's new cosmetics line is an utter disaster, you're unlikely to read a trenchant critique in *Lovely Me* magazine. When I worked on a glossy, in the early 1990s, we'd shoot the cover girl and then simply invent whatever products the make-up artist was supposed to have used on her to match the brand name of the expensive ad on the back cover. So if Dior had spent thousands and thousands advertising on the back, we'd say the make-up used on Miss Supermodel was by Dior. We made it up. Everyone does a blue eyeshadow: the stuff used in the picture may have been by Maybelline, but we'd say it was Bleu Fabuleux, or whatever, by C. Dior. I used to wonder about the poor girl who'd saved up to buy the lipstick Christy Turlington was supposed to be wearing, and who'd ask herself why it looked so different on her.

None of which is to say there aren't excellent beauty writers around, because there are (Newby Hands of *Harpers & Queen* is worth the cover price alone), but they are the exception rather than the rule. It remains a fact that your average beauty article is quite likely to be a clumsy rehash of a press release from some multinational beauty corporation, passing on to you, the reader, only what said multinational wants you to know – i.e. that its product is revolutionary. Yeah, yeah. The nuisance with this is that you get boy who cried wolf syndrome: no doubt some products really are exceptional, but they become lost in the torrent of hysterical praise heaped upon absolutely everything else.

In beauty, like elsewhere, what you really want to know is what works. You are unlikely to find this out from any source that needs megabucks cosmetics advertising revenue to survive. You won't necessarily find it out from me either – my recommendations are, obviously, entirely subjective: they are what works for me. But I'm giving it my best shot – we have a lifetime's findings coming up – so read on; and do also visit the utterly fantastic **www.makeupalley.com** message boards – discussions on everything from really obscure scent to the best red nail polish, from informed, intelligent, literate punters. It gets very addictive. For serious, useful, take-no-prisoners reviews of products, subscribe to Heather Kleinman's Cosmetic Connection at www.cosmeticconnection.com. You'll get a weekly e-mail reviewing a specific line and access to a searchable database of reviews. Kleinman really knows her onions.

There is an especial joy in shopping for make-up and other beauty products: namely, you're never too fat, too short, too thin (oh, boo hoo) – and, given that cheap make-up is very often the business, you are seldom too broke.

You can be too young, though. I was never allowed to wear make-up and my schoolfriends were; at primary school in London, I remember gazing with agonized longing at my friend Catriona's make-up bag – a grubby fluffy pencil case – which represented to me the absolute acme of sophistication. She lived, with her mother and older sister, just down the road from school (we were both at the Lycée in London, but Catriona was English), and her mother – fabulous, with a jet-black beehive, sooty eyes and a dancer's body – would smile indulgently as we played with her make-up. Catriona wore mascara on her huge hyacinth-blue eyes, *and* lipstick, *and* blusher. I was completely bare-faced, and completely envious. I *knew* everything there was to know about make-up, the cosmetics counters exercising as strong a pull as the stationer's, and could tell a Dior lipstick from a Chanel at a hundred paces.

This was in no small part because I had by this time acquired a stepmother, Anne, whose life was devoted to cosmetic enhancement. She took tanning pills, and so had orange palms; she wore frosted eyeshadow of the kind considered unspeakably vulgar by my mother, and three coats of mascara; she had, shall we say, unsubtly streaked hair; she went to the gym before anyone else I knew; she sunbathed topless (I remember being ten and surreptitiously studying her nipples on the beach); she had 'treatments' every day; she was *permanently* on a diet of small yoghurts. Her regime would have killed another kind of woman. I liked her – she was like a creature, and very kind to me. Anne suffered from constipation, and every summer at the seaside, I'd get the breakfast *petits pains* (which she didn't eat – she had an early and morbid fear of carbohydrates) and, on my return, solicitously inquire about her morning evacuations:

– *Ça a été, Anne?*

– *Non. Pas de succès.*

She'd look downcast, so would I, and a gloomy atmosphere would descend upon the breakfast table. (Incidentally, I don't recommend discussing your morning poos over the Frosties. It's really, really unsexy. I want my boyfriend to believe that I'm such a goddess of fox that I don't even *have* bowel movements. This may sound old-fashioned, but I don't care. I have enough male friends to know that companionable poo-chats do little for the male libido. Poo-chats lead to pal-sex – as in, if you were a bloke he'd thwack you appreciatively on the back, but since you're not, he'll go for a half-hearted, matey shag instead.)

Later – much, much later, when Anne had left my father because he ran out of money and had shacked up with a very rich, very fat man (Anne, I mean, not my dad) – the man was the fattest I'd ever met in a double-bed context: it was awful to think of anyone you knew actually doing it with him – I realized that the gold razor blade she wore around her neck wasn't exclusively decorative. I also realized – I was seventeen, and the shock of it practically made me pass out – that my father and she had liked, Frenchly, group sex – swapping, swinging, going to strange sex parties in strange houses. I realized because, over a pre-dinner drink, she cheerfully showed me photographs of these parties – I was, after all, 'an adult now' – flicking the thick pages of the leather-bound album with a manicured finger. She wasn't remotely trying to freak me out, I don't think – she, my father and her new partner, Mr Porky, were all giggling indulgently at the photos, as though to say, 'Goodness, double penetration, weren't we silly.' Then the album went away and we carried on making small talk. I sometimes think I must have imagined this event, but I kept a diary at the time and, having just consulted it, know for a fact that I didn't. Now, I think that people who want to have group sex should go right ahead, and a part of me can absolutely see the appeal; but seeing your father's penis peering out of a photograph is perhaps best avoided if you are a sensitive adolescent. It was absolutely massive, which really didn't help (or perhaps it did: if I have to think about my father's penis, I'd rather it was sizeable than humiliatingly minute, I *suppose*). My father was extremely devoted to sex, as evidenced not only by his marriages, hundreds of girlfriends and so on, but also by his massive collection of pornography. There were thousands of back issues all over his apartment, in neat, orderly piles. He used to read *Playboy* and *Lui* quite casually, as the family gathered for a pre-prandial *aperitif*, which makes me laugh to myself as I type. I love the idea of him making distinctions between what was and what wasn't acceptable reading matter in front of one's great-aunt in one of Europe's most staunchly Catholic countries: *Playboy*, yes, *Anal Sluts*, no.

Anyway, the point is that I wasn't allowed to wear make-up for ages. Eventually, my mother made one small (to her – it was vast to me) concession: I could wear kohl, because it was Indian and so was I. What she didn't quite register, I don't think, was that kohl was, in the mid-1970s, absolutely where it was at eye-wise, and so I whooped with joy, crammed as much of it as I could into my eyes and went off, skipping. The application of kohl sparked a lifelong devotion to every kind of make-up.

After I'd had my first child, I felt like a beached whale for months – a very happy beached whale, but a beached whale none the less. My post-Caesarean stomach, which had been pretty convex even pre-pregnancy, left quite a lot to be desired. Feeling fat, frumpy and mumsy, I got back into make-up big time (this wasn't a first: I spent my teens in sooty false eyelashes and my university career sporting a faux beauty spot just below my left eye. I had the feeling I was rather divinely eight-

eenth century. Oh *dear* – youth). But that's what I
so love about make-up: you may feel like you're
never going to have a normal body again, you may
wince when you sit down, you may be knackered
all the time – but then you go out to dinner wearing glittery green eyeshadow and you feel much
better. Also, unlike the more dramatic forms of
transformation, if it looks crap you can just wash
it off.

The very cornerstone of looking good is, indis-
putably, good skin, which is why there are
hundreds of different foundations, concealers and
bases on the market. Good skin is the nirvana of
make-up. Ironically enough, what all we make-up
junkies want is to have the kind of dermis that
makes make-up an optional extra. What most of
us have to make do with is the kind of skin that's
pretty so-so *au naturel* but not so bad that it can't
be perfectly concealed – that is, given the appear-
ance of perfection – with foundation.

First things first. I'd say, don't go there unless
you absolutely have to, i.e. unless you've tried every
skin-improving cleanser and potion and failed.
Work on the skin first, not on the camouflage. Like
any tricks involving gel-filled breast pads or tinted
contact lenses, covering up your real skin with faux
skin out of a tube means you're only going to
disappoint ultimately (this is a euphemism for 'at
bedtime'). Nobody wants to be the sort of woman

who turns from peach to pasty, blotchy wreck when she washes her face – which is why many of us have slept in foundation every now and then over the years to impress some Mr Lover-Lover or other, even though we knew this was a dermato-logically disastrous course of action. Please don't do this: the foundation smears into the pillow, which makes you look dirty and slapperish; the bits that don't end up in the bedding end up blocking your pores; and, most crucially, slept-in foundation makes doing the Walk of Shame – the getting home the following morning – far more sordid than it need be.

Good skin starts with good cleansing. I really think I've tried them all, the cleansers, over the years, waiting for The One. I finally found it aged thirty-seven, rather in the manner of a Barbara Pym hero-ine finally finding love with a curate. It is called Cleanse and Polish Hot Cloth Cleanser, it is made by the former beauty journalist Liz Earle, it is quasi-organic, and it has totally changed my skin – the dry bits aren't dry any more, the oily bits appear normal, my skin feels squeaky-clean but not tight or stripped, and my face just looks more even, some-how. It's not expensive, either and because Liz Earle works by mail or online ordering, provided you have a phone you can get it by the day after tomorrow even if you live in the Outer Hebrides. You use it with a muslin cloth, which means you don't need to exfoliate separately. (The muslin cloth is where it's at, really, no matter what cleanser you use – buy them cheap in the baby department of any big store, and please wash them after two uses, not, as a friend of mine does, weekly – urgh.)

I don't personally believe in putting dodgy – or even undodgy – chemicals on my (absorbent, porous – der!) skin. I have the kind of skin that flares up dramatically at the smallest provocation. I can't use most normal bubble baths, and if I'm stressed, for instance, I get weird rashes. I'm sure all those creams and potions with magical-sounding proper-ties and names that are supposed to be terribly convincing and scientific work for some people – it's just they don't work for me, and besides I find them obscurely creepy.

I should make special mention here of a cleanser called Cetaphil. This is what you should use if your skin is a disaster, or hypersensitive – if you have eczema, say, or have (sun) burnt yourself, or if you suddenly start developing allergies. It's the cleanser dermatologists recommend for women who've just had plastic surgery: incredibly gentle, but gets every-thing off. The maddening thing about Cetaphil is that it is a timorous beastie and doesn't advertise itself, so you usually have to order it from your chemist – if you tell them it's made by a company called Galderma, they can look it up (and can normally get it in for you within a couple of days).

It's very cheap and comes in an unlovely plastic bottle, but it really does the business. NB: If you're going to the States, Cetaphil is available in every drug store, even cheaper and marginally more attractively packaged (with pump dispenser). I find it too emollient to use every day, because I have combination skin, but if you have dry sensitive skin that hates ordinary cleansers, this is going to be your new best friend.

So, use a decent cleanser, moisturize – but not madly: I've never, for instance, met anyone who needed to moisturize their nose or chin, though I've met lots of people who wonder why they have nose and chin blackheads and otherwise perfect skin – and try to visit a facialist every now and then if you possibly can. It's expensive and self-indulgent, but it really does make a dramatic difference. And again, I implore you, if they seem expensive – which they are – get friends and relatives to club together to book you a treatment. People are far too undemanding about birthdays: a really top facial costs the same as two not especially lovely bottles of scent and a bunch of garage flowers. Or a dinner for two. Which you get is up to you – I'd rather have the peachy skin.

There are all sorts of different facials available. My theory is that, lovely as it is to have your face pummelled and massaged with rose oil, it doesn't actually do a huge amount of good when it comes to seeing the difference a few days later. I like – like is the wrong word: I am *impressed by* (grossly) – extraction facials, where pores are unblocked, rubbish removed with tools, skin squeezed, and you come out with what looks like new skin. To me, having a facial means having a treatment that I couldn't carry out at home myself. Incidentally, assuming you have normal-ish skin, a good facial-ist should leave you radiant and ready to go straight out, not spotty or red or covered in oily unguents. And for goodness' sake, have a look at your facial-ist's skin before lying down, and use your common sense. I once went for a facial in Dickins and Jones which was administered by a woman with throb-bing facial pustules (also she breathed through her mouth, like a rapist). Very sad for her, but really horrid for me. If the products they're using on you aren't working on them, why bother?

So you've got your skin sorted out, we hope (give it at least a month, which is how long it takes for skin cells to renew themselves). It's time to gild the lily.

How to Have Absolutely Perfect-seeming Skin

You've been paying attention, you've been using the right products, your skin is looking way better than it has in the past, and you're happy to do the tinted moisturizer/odd dash of concealer thing most days. But tonight's a big night and you want to look *flawless*. This is what you do (it's not quick, by the way – and not to be attempted anywhere badly lit. Ideally you need one of those Hollywood starlet mirrors, with bulbs all the way around, or harsh daylight. Forty watts and a cracked mirror won't do).

1. Moisturize your skin generously, and then go and read a magazine from cover to cover – we're talking *Heat* rather than the *New Yorker*: fifteen minutes to half an hour is ideal, a wee bit longer is fine. If you put your slap on to a just-moisturized face, it'll slide off. If you put it on dry skin, it'll cake in patches and look weird. You need the moisturizer to do its thing and to sink in properly.

2. I use make-up artist Laura Mercier's line – she, quite rightly, has a bee in her bonnet about 'creating perfect skin', and I heartily recommend her products. If you're using another range (Estée Lauder does excellent foundations, as do Prescriptives), look for equivalents.

On your thirst-quenched, moisturized skin, apply a thin layer of Foundation Primer all over. This is a relatively new product – all the big names do a version – that may very well be yet another ingenious way of getting you to part with your money pointlessly. What it does in theory is create a seal, or barrier, between your moisturized skin and the slap you're about to pile on top. As I say, I do see how people might be sceptical about these primers, but I believe in them. I find they work, provide a smoother base, protect the skin and make the slap last longer.

3. Get a clean cosmetic sponge, run it under the cold tap and squeeze it as hard as you can so that it is only very, very barely damp. Place two little blobs of foundation on the back of your hand. I use Mercier's oil-free foundation, which is very heavily pigmented, so that you need to use only a titchy amount. You get what you pay for with foundation. Do ask about pigment concentration when you're buying yours – there's no point in getting a huge, cheap-seeming bottle that needs three clumsy layers to make any difference. It's like buying watercolours when you want acrylics, or indeed oils. Or stucco.

Work the foundation into your skin, using the sponge, and then work it in again, using your fingers. I find the middle fingers are best – they're more sensitive than the gnarled old indexes. When I say work it in, I mean for minutes rather than seconds, and don't forget your eyelids.

4. You now have much nicer skin, but you still have red bits, or the odd broken capillary, or a spot you need to hide. DO NOT slap on more foundation,

unless you are deliberately going for the trolley-dolly look, or paying your very own homage to Joan Collins. Get out your concealer. This really should be Laura Mercier's utterly stellar Secret Camouflage (which I owned for years without properly under-standing how to use it: ask for a demonstration if you buy it, or for an explanation over the phone). It's expensive, but it lasts for ever (we're back to high levels of pigment), and you could literally hide a port stain with it (though for port stains and their ilk, you might want to try Dermablend, available from, among others, **www.escentual.co.uk**). Mix, mix, mix the two colours until you have matched your skin tone perfectly – this takes a bit of practice and will give you something to do on those long winter evenings when you're bored of reading the whole Booker Prize shortlist. Then pat the mix on to any problematic areas with the little brush, and pat again with a finger. *Voilà!* Miraculously, the concealer has melded with the base without looking remotely obvious – or indeed detectable. Your skin is now perfectly even – you fox, you – and an immaculate blank canvas. But we're not done yet.

5. You will inevitably have some mixed-up concealer left on the back of your hand. Dip the brush into some eye cream and mix a dot of this with a dot of the concealer, and brush and pat microscopic quantities under the eyes. This feels

very nice and fresh, and it gets rid of any shadows (if the shadows are really disastrous, use Touche Éclat as well).

6. You may, at this point, feel that you look a bit matt – a bit too backing singer in Robert Palmer video. Or you may not: it depends on where you're going and what you're planning on doing to the rest of your face. Carry on making up your face and look again when you've finished. If you decide that you'd like a bit of an unmattifying sexy glow, reach for Secret Finish. This is an anodyne-looking white liquid – you squeeze a blob on to your fingers and pat it gently on to your temples, cheekbones and anywhere else you like (go easy, though) for that slightly sheeny, but not iridescent look. It's what they used on Sarah Jessica Parker in *Sex and the City*: it makes your skin look fresh and young and some-how elastic. Whenever I wear this, I get compli-mented on my amazing, naturally fabulous, glowing skin. And I accept the compliments graciously, chortling to myself. It's a truly great product.

How to Look Effortlessly, Classically Chic, Even If You're Crap at Make-up

Very French, this, and sexy, and fabulous. Also time-less. Wear only red-red lipstick – nothing else. This relies on decent skin and careful application, otherwise you look like Courtney Love or some superannuated Goth leftover.

In order to work, this look requires immaculately groomed and shaped brows: they are *crucial*. As is having lips: this doesn't work if you have a slit for a mouth, like a tadpole. If you don't want or don't need to go for the full foundation monty, as described above, just wear tinted moisturizer and concealer where needed – or go bare: all the attention is on your mouth and eyes, not on the odd blemish. You could, I suppose, add a minute slick of mascara, but absolutely nothing else. Works with all colourings and all skin tones, and men *love* it. But get the red right, for heaven's sake – it doesn't work with orange or pink or burgundy. We're talking red-red, as in pillar box, fire engine, sinful apple. Oh, the glamour.

How to Make Yourself Look Pulled-together in a Hurry

Light base, as above. Blusher – we're after big, rosy cheeks rather than stripy carmine streaks. Flat, blunt, thin eyeshadow brush. Dampen and dip blunt edge into dark – navy, brown, black – eyeshadow. Open eye; pull up eyelid. Look down. Using brush, pat the damp shadow *inside* your top lid, from the outside in, from corner to corner. Less harsh or obvious than kohl or liquid eyeliner, but makes eye look 'finished' and defined. Mascara. Vaseline for lips.

How to Make Yourself Look at Least Ten Years Older, and Like You've Been Round the Block a Few Times

Ordinary black eyeliner, unsmudged, in two harsh lines, top and bottom. I mean under the lashes, not inside the actual lid, on the bottom. This is a total, total disaster, unless you're in your early twenties, tops, and going for that Gettys in Marrakech look (and even then, this isn't the best way to achieve it). On anyone else – and that probably means you – it is *calamitous*. It's very, very hard, for starters – hard enough to be actively butch (which is why eyeliner worn this way suits most men). And then it closes the eye and makes it look small and avian, like the eye of a horrible mean bird, e.g. a crow, that pecks at corpses. Also, for some reason, even if this and mascara are all you're wearing, you look like you're wearing a ton of make-up: I've lost count of the number of times people have said, 'She wears too much make-up' of some poor woman sporting this hideous look and nothing else. No, unsmudged eyeliner, top and bottom, is

a look that reminds me of beefy fifty-year-old pros-
titutes in Newcastle, with big chins and giant
hands. Most women wear it as a matter of course
from their thirties onwards, even though it looks
horrible and makes them look ancient and birdy.
Are they *blind*?

Eyeliner *inside* both top and bottom lids is fine,
especially if you have long, almondy eyes. If you
don't, I really wouldn't bother: it's not especially
flattering. Smudged eyeliner top and bottom is OK,
but only if you're deliberately going for the houri
look. Smudged top only is good on everyone.
Round eyes are good with impeccably applied
flicky liquid eyeliner: very *Dolce Vita*. Flicky eyeliner
on eyes that aren't round doesn't usually work – it
makes them incredibly small. I suppose some
people admire Renée Zellwegger's micro-peepers,
but I'm not one of them.

How to Make Yourself Look Naturally Alluring and More Awake

Buy some heated eyelash curlers. Yes, they do make
a difference, and the newest, battery-operated
versions (a selection of which is available from
www.missgroovy.co.uk – I like the Mr Mascara
ones) seem less like a medieval instrument of
torture than their predecessors. Failing these, heat

old-fashioned curlers with a hairdryer before apply-
ing. Either way, use an eyelash comb, available from
all chemists for about a quid. (I can't understand
why the eyelash comb isn't a universally used
device. All mascaras, no matter how good, cause
some clumping, and who needs clumps?)

Obviously, you can't have the lovely face and let
it all go to rack and ruin from the neck down. But
I don't have any particular recommendations here:
I wash with Liz Earle bath wash, or with Dove
soap, and, more often than not, wash my hair with
the children's cherry-almond-flavoured shampoo,
which comes in a pleasing container shaped like a
fish. I don't use body lotion, except sometimes on
my legs, and have very soft skin none the less,
though I say so myself – I think it's because I've
never used it in my life, and my skin has adjusted
accordingly. Children don't use body lotion, after
all, and they have delicious peachy skin. The more
I think about it, the more I decide that body lotion,
though pleasant enough, is a total swizz. In dermis
extremis – wintry elbows emerging in the spring,
and so on – you can't go wrong with Palmer's
Cocoa Butter: it's cheap, you don't need much and
it seems to work overnight.

Hair is a different story. My life has been trans-
formed by finding the right hairdresser: again, this
happened very late in my life. I have curly hair,
which hairdressers used to love to turn into a sort

of big, poodly Afro – they'd stand back, clap their hands with delight and shout, 'Do you *love* it?', as though it were every girl's dream to look exactly like Bruno Martelli from *Fame*. Or they'd make it totally flat and straight, à la Morticia, except with my round face peering out sadly from behind the gloomy black curtains. Then I met Richard, and everything changed. I can't make you meet Richard, alas, but I can encourage you to be *brutal* in your discussions with hairstylists. You need to explain exactly what you want, and to be just as explicit about what you don't. If, mid-cut, you feel alarmed, don't just tell yourself that the stylist knows what s/he's doing and that it's all bound to turn out all right. It isn't. Voice your concerns. Know your limitations, though, and don't be a pain in the arse: if your hair is fine, no stylist is going to give you thick, tumbling locks.

And then there are the other bits. The compelling pop gossip website popbitch (**www.popbitch.com**) has a fixation with Madonna's supposedly gnarled and aged hands. I haven't had the chance to get a good look, but it is certainly true – and getting gruesomely truer, what with Botox and its ilk – that some women with oddly youthful faces have startlingly unyouthful, claw-like hands. There isn't much you can do about age spots and the like, apart from being zapped by lasers. I've witnessed a friend having a course of these laser treatments

– pulse-light therapy, it was called – which seemed to work, but I found the whole process terrifying to watch and wouldn't have it done to myself in a million years.

What you can, and should, do is massage your hands with a nourishing cream (Palmer's Cocoa Butter, as above, is excellent) and either have professional manicures or give yourself them at home. Having said that, some people just have really odd hands – I am thinking particularly of women who have adult-sized hands but with children's tiny, friable fingernails: quite freaky – and all the manicures and polish in the world isn't going to help them. Pity, really, that gloves aren't more fashionable. But you could always start a trend.

Pedicures are a different thing altogether. They are crucial, and, thank goodness, proper pedicurists are finally appearing in Britain. God knows what took them this long: in Paris, or in Brussels, you can go and have a *pedicure medicale* pretty much anywhere. Given that we're on our feet all day and that we have only one pair, it stands to reason that we should take care of them, by which I do not mean simply painting the toes pretty colours and pushing back the cuticles. I mean serious, heavy-duty stuff that's too unsexy to describe but that leaves you feeling like somebody has very kindly given you new tootsies. Do visit your chiropodist: they're not just for old biddies with corns, you know – and anyway, if you get in there early enough, you'll never *be* an old biddy with corns.

Working our way back up, we come to the middle bit. Yes, the, um, mons. I know, it's not romantic – and it's not entirely on-subject either. But it's my book, so might I just make a tiny little plea? Having all your pubic hair waxed away is really, really *weird*. By all means, have it tidied up if you are naturally hirsute, or have it topiaried, within reason. But the recent fashion for either a landing strip or having nothing there at all is extremely bizarre. I understand you need to act if you're going to wear a minute bikini, but that kind of waxing still falls within normal realms. What's with having it all off? To put it bluntly, it makes you look like a child. Why would you want your genitals to look like a child's, exactly? Because your boyfriend likes it? Get a new boyfriend, is my advice. Because it makes the area more sensitive? Well, so would tenderizing it with a meat mallet first. I mean, come on. No healthy person's nerve endings are that faulty.

Mothers and Children

Ah, the little darlings. When my sister Amaryllis had just started school and was learning to write, she penned the following:

> God who macs the sky
> God who makes the art
> Evrything above
> Are gret
> God who macs the clauds
> God who macs the fich
> God who make the CHOPS
> Are grat!

A remarkable little verse, I think we'd all agree: you can just feel all the tremulous excitement of the last line (she was only five at the time), talk about eloquence – if not spelling. This says it all, really. My mother didn't drag my little sisters out shopping with her for ages, and then, inevitably, one day she did. The results, as seen in the above poem, were cataclysmic. Children love The Shops, with a passion and an all-devouring hunger that are both terrifying: they want everything. What do you do? We've all seen

– we've all had – children that fling themselves about on the floor because you are disinclined to buy them yet another horrible bit of primary-coloured plastic or bag of tooth-rotting sweeties in the shape of aliens. You blush with shame, and go all prickly about the armpits, because there are always people watching, and every single one of them is thinking 'spoilt brat' – a very hypocritical reaction, but a universal one none the less. So your own response becomes ridiculous: you either try and have a rational discussion, in the manner of Isaiah Berlin and Richard Rorty discussing the limits of pragmatism; or you lose your temper in a completely disproportionate way, and end up buying the wretched thing to atone for having just had an epi at a three-year-old child.

I think we do indulge our children to a really ludicrous extent: they more or less have everything they want, whether they're with you at the supermarket, merrily piling the trolley high with Frosties and toxic-looking cakes, or you're at The Shops proper and don't see how buying another Playmobil figure is really going to do very much harm – plus, it's bound to keep them quiet over lunch (plus, well, it's Playmobil, innit. It's *educational*, in a way: not trash. See also Lego). When I worked in an office, as opposed to at home, I was always coming back with some trinket or other – really I might as well have been a Victorian suitor, attaching a note about how the enclosed was a humble token of my esteem. I thought it made me a better parent, to keep giving them this *stuff*, because they'd be bound to see how much I thought about them all day and how much I loved them. They were aged three and six months.

Nevertheless, I carried merrily on in this manner for ages – years – even though I'd stopped going out to work. And then one day I realized, as we all do at some point, that 98 per cent of the toys the children had were never played with, and just sat on shelves, looking mournful. That's the thing about having an embarrassment of choice, especially if you're small: you just stick to Blue Bunny or your train set, and are perfectly happy doing so.

So then I culled: heaps and heaps of toys were dropped off at local schools, nurseries, hospitals and hospices (though not books: I always say yes if I'm asked to buy books, no matter how dire or barely literate, on the basis that anything at all that creates an interest in reading is emphatically A Good Thing). I've been culling ever since, twice a year – though now, of course, the children help me by actively participating in the cull. Howls of protest initially, but not any more: the boys are now old enough to understand, and be (temporarily) appalled by, the fact that some children don't have any toys at all. Culls, by the way, are great: I cull my own wardrobe twice a year, and the house's contents. It's one thing to be acquisitive and another to just sit there like a pig wallowing in excess mud. And after the culls you feel community-spirited and decent, for about three seconds.

I think this is the only reasonable response to the tide of toys that otherwise keeps on coming. Just as my house is always drowning in paper, no matter how hard I try to wade through it every now and then – newspapers, magazines, notes, manuscripts, book proofs, letters, bills, bills, bills – so the children's bedroom becomes awash with toys even weeks after one of the culls: swapped toys, pocket money toys, presents. Which reminds me: it is quite hard to get excited about presents if you're bought everything you ever want.

This is not to suggest that children should be forced to play with twigs and pebbles, give or take the odd peg dolly. But I do think that, if you have the kind of overstocked playroom that is more like a toy shop than part of a family house, you are making a rod to break everyone's back with – your children's as well as your own. It is tempting, of course, if you are time-poor and cash-rich, to express your devotion by the ceaseless purchasing of unnecessary toys – but it doesn't work: it creates brats, *always and without exception*.

Of course, shopping with small children is actually not that much of a nightmare compared to the total horror of shopping with teenagers. I am going on my own behaviour here: my children are still too young (though both can do a passable impression of a stroppy fifteen-year-old. Not as well as me, however). I was an utter nightmare to shop with: I was foul, and I wanted stuff. It's a monstrously unattractive combination, that. It's one thing to be foul and sit in your bedroom in Gothic gloom, and another to be foul round and round and up and down and in and out of Brent Cross shopping centre.

I've been fascinated by department stores since I was small, a fascination that was dramatically amplified after reading Zola's *Au Bonheur des Dames* during one particularly *longueurs*-packed Belgian holiday. The novel is about an eponymous nineteenth-century department store, and contrasts the triumphant emergence of capitalist economy and Parisian bourgeois society with the slow, cruel decline of a dusty draper's shop, whose misfortune it is to be situated opposite the gleaming new monolith. Which is making the novel sound ghastly even to me – thank God I'm not a book critic – but it's not; it's a complete page-turner about the consumer society, greed, fashion and instant gratification.

Brent Cross shopping centre was a precursor to Bluewater and its ilk: all the debatable goodness of the American shopping mall brought to north London, with dozens and dozens of shops under one roof. There was a John Lewis, with a particularly well-stocked hosiery department – rows and

rows of 99p Christian Dior tights in puce, bright
yellow, electric blue – a Miss Selfridge (swoon), a
huge Marks & Spencer, and it was between these
three that my poor mother and I (inevitably mutin-
ous, and wearing too many earrings) lurched. Oh,
and there was C&A. Just before I left for boarding
school, my mother and stepfather took me to C&A
and bought me a polka-dotted yellow dress. It had
a fitted bodice, a wide smocked waist and a straight-
ish skirt. This was the dress I wore with the crimi-
nal non-mufti pale blue socks for my first dinner at
my new school. It sticks in my head like glue.

My mother also liked taking me to M&S, which
I was prejudiced against enough to really crank up
the eye rolling and desperate sighing over.
Presumably, perfectly reasonably, she wanted to get
whatever I needed in between stocking up on
Babygros (she had two small daughters) and eggs,
and didn't see why M&S should be considered such
a hardship by me.

She developed quite a crafty technique, my
mum: she'd hold up some unexciting garment or
other and say, 'Oh! How absolutely amazing! Can
it really be . . . Why, yes. This is a *direct* copy of
Saint Laurent! Look, India. Look at the neckline!
Look at the red, like . . . garnets gleaming in the
sun.' This worked once or twice, when some dress
she was holding up did indeed, somehow, trans-
form itself through the miracle of good cutting

from drab on the hanger to fab on the body – though I think it is perhaps overly optimistic to believe that the designers at M&S, talented as they no doubt were, scoured the Parisian catwalk for their designs and ripped off the secrets of aged seamstresses in couture *ateliers*.

Nevertheless, emboldened by her success, my mother took to employing the Saint Laurent Method on all M&S clothes, from pants (in the knicker sense) to warm, cosy anoraks ('Pure Givenchy! How do they do it?'). She also, to my utter and crippling mortification, insisted that I try things on there and then, on the Marks & Spencer floor, saying, at the top of her voice, that no one would look, since no one was remotely interested in my thighs. Writing this, I am actually trying to remember whether M&S had changing rooms at all: I'm thinking that perhaps they didn't, and that perhaps this purgatorial ritual was commonplace, though I don't remember anyone else, crimson with shame, standing in their pants and tights for those few seconds before stepping into the proffered pair of trousers, surrounded by happy shoppers and – always – Hassidim. (I especially remember the Hassidim because my mother has fairly robust views on Palestine, which she is not shy about sharing, then or now. Over the years, some of these trips to Brent Cross became occasions to educate me about the Middle East. I'd say, 'Mummy, shush. *We're surrounded by Orthodox Jews,*' and she'd say, 'Good. I absolutely love Jews. It's just the Israelis I can't stand').

If you were wearing a skirt, obviously, you could pull the new skirt on underneath, but for some reason I was always wearing trousers, and trousers ('Dior copies! The brilliance!') were what I needed to try on. You don't see that many fourteen-year-olds in their pants standing scarlet-faced in the middle of M&S any more. I was a pioneer.

This calvary with the pants and the Hassidim was necessary, because I knew that if I complied in M&S, we'd maybe get to go to Miss Selfridge afterwards. Miss Selfridge was the promised land, with its mannequins in spiky fluorescent wigs, its hangers dripping with tight, low-cut things, not in colours like sun-drenched garnets but in BLACK: skirts that looked like spider's webs, vaguely Goth tops, short skirts, tight T-shirts . . . heaven. Well, heaven for me – only sometimes heaven for my mother. And I do see her problem here: from a relatively early age, one of my sartorial role models has been the prostitute (glamorized ideal of) – not so much now, as I approach forty, but in my prime. This was partly to do with having a raving beauty as a mother – a raving, impeccably elegant beauty, whose look I knew I could never successfully approximate. My mother is small and I am five foot ten; she has an elegant little bosom, whereas mine is wench-like; she is classically beautiful with amazing bone structure, whereas I am OK; she is skinny-pinny, I am not. And anyway, no teenager wants to look like their mum, no matter how ravingly gorgeous. Besides, I'd spent my childhood sweetly dressed as Little Miss Square; time, surely, for a change. I think my teenage devotion to working-girl chic may also have had to do with my father's porno mags: the only women I knew with busts like mine were in those magazines, looking not entirely wholesome (unless they were reclining on straw, pretending to be farmers) but clearly desirable none the less.

But it is to my mother's tremendous credit that she never actually refused to buy me the clothes I liked; or actively stopped me from wearing them out and about. When I dyed my hair white (no mean feat if it's black to start off with), she said it made my eyes greener. When I decided to get myself tattooed as a seventeenth-birthday present to myself, she dissuaded me from choosing anything too gruesome as an image, but not from the tattoo itself. In earlier years, she'd occasionally look quite cross – once, in Laura Ashley of all places, she pretended she wasn't with me – at whatever I'd decided to wear, but she never actually said, 'No way' or 'Take it off.'

And this is part of the miracle of shopping: sometimes, when she and I hadn't exchanged a civil word in days, I'd try something on in Miss Selfridge, my mother waiting impatiently outside, looking thunderous, and as I came out, her whole face would

What to Wear If You're Not a Size 12

I fall into this category myself, so this advice is from the heart.

1. Don't, whatever you do, buy baggy Fat People's Clothes. THIS IS CRUCIAL. All designers make these – they are very, very loose, flowing things, usually waistless, that look amazing if you're a size 10, because the whole point of them is the contrast between voluminous fabric and skinny body. Tragically, larger women tend not to understand this and, delighted that they have finally found things that fit after hours of traipsing around Selfridges feeling depressed, jubilantly get out their credit card. The result is disastrous: you end up looking unimaginably vast, and like you're wearing a gigantic sack. Also, these clothes make your head look tiny – we're talking diplodocus, really. You want things with waists, even if you think yours is non-existent, and you definitely don't want anything that fits loosely on the bosom and then goes all flowy: I can absolutely guarantee that you'll look heavily pregnant. What I'm saying is, buy clothes that fit, not clothes that are too loose, no matter how tempting these seem. You probably have a good bust; show it off. You're probably curvy; ditto. Don't sausage yourself into a Spandex tube, but do wear a little cardigan that

fits, and a long straight skirt (beware excess fabric, around the waist or elsewhere – anything gathered or pleated will make you look like Pregnant Mrs Big Arse).

2. Never, ever wear those heavy, knitted cotton jumpers. There's something very appealing about these, in a 'Let's pretend it's Fall in Connecticut' way, but they add on a couple of dress sizes and make any bosoms bigger than a C cup – or maybe even a B – look absolutely bovine, and any shoulders that aren't narrow look like a shotputter's. Go for wool, silk or cashmere instead. Bulky tops are a disaster – if you're worried about being chilly (unlikely: you have plenty of insulation), carry a shawl around with you.

3. Avoid high necks, particularly with T-shirts, if your bosom is anything other than small. Round-necked T-shirts with a big bust make you look like your breasts start just below your neck and don't really ever end. V-necks, please, as low as you like (within reason). The exception to this is the trusty cashmere cardi – but unbuttoned.

4. What you wear underneath is of the utmost importance. Get a good bra and Pants of Steel for special occasions. This can make the most spectacular difference.

5. Bottoms. Mine isn't vast, but I know some that are. In my experience, these are better displayed than covered up. Having a flap of fabric over your big bottom is not flattering; in some instances, it can make people look deformed from the waist down. Show that bottom! Yes, some people might think, 'Blimey, look at her arse – it's huge.' But for every person who does, somebody else will be thinking, 'Fwoar! I am powerfully reminded of J-Lo, and I have the horn.'

6. Stomachs. Grim, innit? Mine is horrendous from two C-sections and no sit-ups. I don't think there's any disguising miracle, stomach-wise – alas. The old Pants of Steel do help, though. I just show my breasts quite a lot and hope that no one's eye travels downwards too much. Try also praying to St Jude, the patron saint of lost causes.

7. Where to shop . . . Anything from Ghost, especially long bias-cut skirts. Wrap dresses from Diane von Furstenberg (very flattering, sexy – stockists from www.dvf.com; try also www.net-a-porter.com). Maharishi 'pants' (also net-a-porter). Boden for pottering about in. Designers at Debenhams – you occasionally stumble upon a marvel. Topshop's Tall Girl range if you're, er, tall – marvellous long denim skirts with stretch.

soften and she'd say, 'That really suits you' or 'Oh, how lovely' or 'And you could wear the new strappy sandals with it.' She is not what you'd call a conciliatory type, my mother: she wasn't trying to be sweet to make up for some earlier argument. She was genuinely pleased that I looked nice in whatever it was I'd tried on, and was genuinely saying so. And there would be a cessation of hostilities for, ooh, hours sometimes.

So actually, after I'd got over the slouching around looking grumpy and the rolling of eyes, I came to the conclusion that shopping wasn't half useful when it came to what we'd now call bonding. Even in Sainsbury's: too horrid and teenage to say, 'Sorry, and can we be friends now?' I'd pick up some new thing and show it to her, and our common greed would allow us to speak normally to each other while discussing the virtues of, say, undyed haddock. To this day, my mother and I are at utter peace with one another when shopping, whether we're scrutinizing a *pâtisserie* display, trying to choose a cake for tea, or buying shoes together. I am puzzled by those very expensive Tesco ads that showed Jane Horrocks as the daughter and Prunella Scales as the mother, bickering and exasperating each other round the supermarket. In my experience, when push comes to shove, women shopping together – any kind of shopping, any kind of women – always leads to some kind of ceasefire.

New in Store

Old habits die hard, and I keep coming across new places which didn't find themselves into the original edition of *The Shops*. Here are some of them. It's a bit of a hotch-potch of a list, but every single place is most heartily recommended.

Philosophy The Supernaturals is the only daytime lipstick anyone ever needs – it looks like you've been eating cherries and then rushed out with your mouth still stained. It comes with a wand, and is superior to all other lip stains you might have tried, not least for ease and precision of application. Add lipgloss and you've got the perfect evening pout. Available from a number of places, including . . .

www.hqhair.com possibly the best beauty site in the UK. From hard-to-find specialist lines like Dermalogica (who, in my opinion, do the best, complexion-changing cleansers) and Terax (no-nonsense Italian hair products, a godsend if you have curly hair) to costume jewellery and electrical goods, this is a brilliant place to browse. It's also excellent if you're looking for presents for your girlfriends (or yourself, natch).

www.bloom.uk.com do the most amazing fake flowers. I know, I know – fake flowers make you want to barf, pause and then barf again. But wait: check these out first. Every bloom is botanically correct (and apparently even fools bees), so that you get the odd manky leaf or worm-hole. The flowers themselves are simply exquisitely beautiful, and the stunning informal arrangements have something of the still life about them. Particularly amazing are the full-blown old-fashioned roses, though really every page has something dazzling and artful. I can't stop buying them – and yes, everybody is fooled. Listen, I gave some of these to the editor of *Wallpaper** magazine, and he absolutely loves them – that's how cool they are. Again, they make brilliant presents.

A total lifesaver when I was last pregnant was **www.9london.co.uk**, who only stock fabulous clothes. Not just okay clothes that'll do *faute de mieux*, but really drop-dead-gorgeous kit that you'll wish you could wear even after the sproglet has dropped. There are Chip & Pepper jeans, for instance, which are perfection, DVF dresses, Homemummy loungewear, including the brilliant Go Anywhere Dress, Melissa Odabash swimwear –

the list goes on and on, in a very Notting Hill chic kind of way. A really wonderful site (or you can ring them and go and see them), that'll make you feel like a fashion goddess even when you're eight months gone and suffering from chronic piles.

Stockings and tights from **www.mytights.co.uk**. Who has the time to shop for hosiery in shops? The selection here is fantastic and they come the next day.

Moomins from **www.moominshop.com**. I love the gloomy Nordic Moomins; I wish I could have one as a pet. Lovely nostalgic presents for small children.

www.emilyreadettbayley.com will sort you out on the home accessories front: painted or gilded wooden letters, shell tableware, feather dusters, driftwood furniture – it's all here, and it's all charming.

Or try **www.re-foundobjects.com**, and download their eccentric, eclectic collection of beautiful (and useful) objects. The shop itself is in Northumberland, but they do mail order. There honestly isn't an object in the entire catalogue that I wouldn't love to have. And none of it is terribly expensive, either.

I can't believe I left Graham & Green out of the original edition. Happily for me, I now live around the corner from one of their shops; happily for you, they have a website: **www.grahamandgreen.co.uk**. This is an absolute treasure trove of deeply desirable and beautiful accessories for the home, plus lovely jewellery, lighting, furniture, mirrors, you name it. And a tiny but very good children's section. I practically live in Graham & Green, it's so wonderful.

I'm trying to relearn to play the piano, and am very pleased to have discovered **www.musicroom.com**, who are a sort of Amazon of sheet music. If you wake up on a Monday feeling like playing a bit of Cole Porter but don't have the music, click on to the site and they'll dispatch it forthwith. They seem to have everything one's musical heart might desire. A truly brilliant site, responsible for a little pile of pieces, that are much too hard for me to play, quietly growing by the side of the piano.

If you have a house rabbit and want to buy it some presents, go to **www.bunnybites.com**. It will thank you.

www.themuseum.co.uk sells those lovely fat 70s (how appropriate) telephones – you know, curly leads and brrring-brrring ringtone. I am very disgruntled with modern phones. Why are they all so hideous? These aren't, and they work perfectly – just plug into any BT socket.

Not so sexy, this one, but it's so miraculous I have
to put it in: if you ever find yourself with a weird
rash on your hands (or anywhere else, for that
matter), and nothing shifts it, try Urtica cream
from Ainsworth Homeopathic Pharmacy, 36 New
Cavendish Street, London W1M 7LH (phone: 020 7935
5330). I get the most hideous skin rashes when I'm
stressed – sometimes it gets so bad that even bath
water stings. This cream sorts me out in about
twenty-four hours. I've treated all three of my children with homeopathic products for small ailments,
including teething (and this worked where all else
had failed). Ainsworth's have a royal warrant (oo err!)
and couldn't be more helpful if they tried: you can
ring them up with symptoms and they'll put a
remedy (which usually costs well under a fiver) in
the post the same day. I know homeopathy makes
some people roll their eyes, but it's so wonderful for
babies and children – it just treats everything without the need for any ghastly drugs or chemicals. Take
the weird questions you'll be asked seriously: your
answers are crucial to them prescribing the right
remedy. You can also buy everything online at
www.ainsworths.com. Give it a go the next time you
have a teething baby – I swear it works.

POCKET PENGUINS

36. **Muriel Spark** The Snobs
37. **Steven Pinker** Hotheads
38. **Tony Harrison** Under the Clock
39. **John Updike** Three Trips
40. **Will Self** Design Faults in the Volvo 760 Turbo
41. **H. G. Wells** The Country of the Blind
42. **Noam Chomsky** Doctrines and Visions
43. **Jamie Oliver** Something for the Weekend
44. **Virginia Woolf** Street Haunting
45. **Zadie Smith** Martha and Hanwell
46. **John Mortimer** The Scales of Justice
47. **F. Scott Fitzgerald** The Diamond as Big as the Ritz
48. **Roger McGough** The State of Poetry
49. **Ian Kershaw** Death in the Bunker
50. **Gabriel García Márquez** Seventeen Poisoned Englishmen
51. **Steven Runciman** The Assault on Jerusalem
52. **Sue Townsend** The Queen in Hell Close
53. **Primo Levi** Iron Potassium Nickel
54. **Alistair Cooke** Letters from Four Seasons
55. **William Boyd** Protobiography
56. **Robert Graves** Caligula
57. **Melissa Bank** The Worst Thing a Suburban Girl Could Imagine
58. **Truman Capote** My Side of the Matter
59. **David Lodge** Scenes of Academic Life
60. **Anton Chekhov** The Kiss
61. **Claire Tomalin** Young Bysshe
62. **David Cannadine** The Aristocratic Adventurer
63. **P. G. Wodehouse** Jeeves and the Impending Doom
64. **Franz Kafka** The Great Wall of China
65. **Dave Eggers** Short Short Stories
66. **Evelyn Waugh** The Coronation of Haile Selassie
67. **Pat Barker** War Talk
68. **Jonathan Coe** 9th & 13th
69. **John Steinbeck** Murder
70. **Alain de Botton** On Seeing and Noticing